BATMAN
THE BRAVE AND THE BOLD ™

TRIO OF TERROR

written by Tracey West
Batman created by Bob Kane

Grosset & Dunlap
An Imprint of Penguin Group (USA) Inc.

PICK YOUR PATH #2

GROSSET & DUNLAP
Published by the Penguin Group
Penguin Group (USA) Inc., 375 Hudson Street, New York,
New York 10014, USA
Penguin Group (Canada), 90 Eglinton Avenue East, Suite 700, Toronto,
Ontario M4P 2Y3, Canada (a division of Pearson Penguin Canada Inc.)
Penguin Books Ltd., 80 Strand, London WC2R 0RL, England
Penguin Group Ireland, 25 St. Stephen's Green, Dublin 2, Ireland
(a division of Penguin Books Ltd.)
Penguin Group (Australia), 250 Camberwell Road, Camberwell,
Victoria 3124, Australia (a division of Pearson Australia Group Pty. Ltd.)
Penguin Books India Pvt. Ltd., 11 Community Centre, Panchsheel Park,
New Delhi–110 017, India
Penguin Group (NZ), 67 Apollo Drive, Rosedale, North Shore 0632,
New Zealand (a division of Pearson New Zealand Ltd.)
Penguin Books (South Africa) (Pty.) Ltd., 24 Sturdee Avenue, Rosebank,
Johannesburg 2196, South Africa

Penguin Books Ltd., Registered Offices:
80 Strand, London WC2R 0RL, England

ISBN 978-0-448-45564-8   10 9 8 7 6 5 4 3 2 1

"Don't step any closer, Batman, or I'll show you a fireworks display you'll never forget!"

The villain Firefly is standing on a crate of fireworks in the middle of the Gotham Fireworks Factory. He's wearing an all-black skintight suit that covers his face entirely. It's fireproof—a necessity when your weapon of choice is a flamethrower.

"Didn't your mother ever tell you not to play with fire?" you ask.

You and your friend Aquaman arrived on the scene as soon as you got word that an intruder had entered the fireworks factory. It's almost the Fourth of July, and the place is filled with huge stacks of crates containing the colorful explosives.

"But, Batman, fire is such a blast!" Firefly replies. "And these fireworks will add a whole new dimension to my arsenal."

"Not if I can help it," you tell him.

"And I, too, will stop you!" Aquaman says boldly.

You need a plan—fast. Firefly is clutching the barrel of his flamethrower. It's attached to two large fuel tanks on his back. If he unleashes it, the fireworks factory will explode in mere seconds.

Then it hits you. You can throw a sharp, bat-shaped throwing star at the tube connecting the flamethrower to the fuel tanks. You quickly slip the throwing star out of your Utility Belt and send it flying toward Firefly.

But the villain has quick reflexes.

"Oh well. Guess I'll just burn the place down!" Firefly threatens.

He ignites his flamethrower before your blade can make contact, and an orange stream of fire shoots out. Once it hits the crates of fireworks, a chain reaction will begin that will be impossible to stop.

Luckily, Aquaman has quick reflexes, too. He aims his sharp-pointed spear at a water pipe overhead. The pipe bursts, splashing water on everything below. Firefly's flame sizzles out—just as the throwing star hits its mark, disabling the weapon for good.

"Noooooo!" Firefly wails. Without his fiery weapon, he's not much of a threat.

You shoot a Batarang with a rope attached at him. The rope wraps around him, binding his arms. You and Aquaman race up to make sure he doesn't get away.

Minutes later, Firefly is cuffed at his wrists and ankles and is being carted away by Gotham City police officers.

You leave him with a parting shot:

"Looks like you'll have some time to cool down now, Firefly."

Then you and Aquaman exit the fireworks factory and emerge into the bright summer day.

"Thank you, Aquaman," you tell your friend. "In the end, water always beats fire."

"It was nothing, old chum," Aquaman says, his massive chest puffed up with pride. "And now I must return to my ocean kingdom. What a tale I have to tell. I shall call it, 'The Tale of the Weird Bug Guy with the Fire Stick'!"

Aquaman leaves, and you turn into the dark alley where you've parked your Batmobile. To your surprise, you see a figure in a trench coat leaning against the hood.

"There'd better not be a scratch on that, Smitty," you say.

Smitty is one of your informants. He's average height, average weight, and has a perfectly average face, which makes him perfectly forgettable. Even his own mother doesn't recognize him when she bumps into him at the grocery store.

But that invisibility makes Smitty a great informant. He can slip in and out of bad guy hangouts without being noticed. He overhears lots of useful information that way—and for a price, he'll share it with you.

Smitty nervously backs away from the Batmobile.

"Sorry, Batman," he tells you. "I've been waitin' a long time. And what I got to tell you is big. Fifty smackers big."

"Let's hear it," you say, curious.

"It's like this," Smitty begins. "The Joker, the Penguin, and the Riddler are each planning something. Word is they're having a contest to see which one of them can pull off the biggest crime without you stoppin' them."

At first, you're not sure if you should believe Smitty. The whole thing sounds crazy—but then again, the Joker, the Penguin, and the Riddler aren't exactly the sanest citizens of Gotham City.

"What kind of proof do you have?" you ask.

Smitty shrugs. "Just talk, Batman. Lots of chatter. But everybody's sayin' the same thing."

Then the police radio on your belt begins to crackle.

"We've got an armed robbery in progress! The Penguin is robbing Gotham First National Bank."

Smitty grins. "Told ya, Batman."

The radio crackles again.

"Ten-four on that. But we've got another problem on the east side. The Riddler is threatening to pull the plug on the Yum-O Ice Cream Factory!"

You shake your head. It sounds like Smitty is right. And there's more.

"We just got an alert from the FBI, boys. Two prominent nuclear scientists have been kidnapped. The Feds think the Joker did it. They're looking for the missing scientists in Gotham City."

You slip a fifty-dollar bill into Smitty's palm.

"Thanks for the tip," you say. Thanks to

Smitty, you know why the three villains are acting up.

"Whatcha gonna do, Batman?" Smitty asks. "How's one guy like you gonna take down three bad guys?"

It's a good question. You think quickly. The villains are pulling you in three different directions. The ice cream factory will have to wait. Someone could get hurt in a bank robbery and the kidnappings of the nuclear scientists worry you—the Joker could be planning something very serious.

If you go after the Penguin first, turn to page 18.
If you go after the Joker first, turn to page 26.

Continued from page 66.

You take a collapsible shield from your Utility Belt. It expands to protect your head and chest. You jump in front of Bronze Tiger to shield him.

It's a good move. This time, snowflake-shaped throwing stars shoot from the umbrella. They clang against the shield and then drop harmlessly to the ground.

The Penguin frowns and drops his umbrella. "Why do you have to be such a pest, Batman?" he moans.

He waddles toward the van to make his getaway. But he isn't known for his speed. While Bronze Tiger keeps the henchmen at bay, you charge up and hold the Penguin's arms behind his back. Then you close your own set of cuffs around his wrists.

"Game over, Penguin," you say.

You get on your radio to contact the police, but all you hear is the sound of crackling static.

"What's wrong, Batman?" Bronze Tiger asks.

"I'm not sure," you reply.

The Penguin starts to cackle. "I may not have won, Batman. But something tells me you're about to lose."

Puzzled, you drag the Penguin to your Batmobile and try your car radio. It's not working. Now people are spilling out onto the street, and they're confused and angry.

"I've got no TV signal!"

"My cell phone won't work!"

"It's a total communication blackout!"

This is bad. If panic keeps rising, Gotham City will be in real trouble. You're not sure what's happening, but you have a feeling that the Joker is behind it.

"I should have gone after the Joker first," you mutter.

THE END

Continued from page 60.

Zatanna doesn't need you to shield her—she's a super hero, and, besides, it looks like she's going to cast a spell. You don't want to get in the way.

Instead, you hit the floor to avoid the projectiles.

"LLAF DNA EB SSELPLEH!" Zatanna cries.

All of the flower projectiles stop whirring and clatter to the floor. When Zatanna casts a spell, she says verbal commands backward. She's just commanded the flowers to "fall and be helpless," and that's exactly what happened. You're impressed.

You jump to your feet. "Good work, Zatanna."

She looks around warily. "Those were easy. I'm worried about what else the Joker might have in store."

"There's one way to find out," you say. "When I was on the floor, I saw the outline of a trapdoor by the stage."

Zatanna nods. "Let's do it."

You open the trapdoor and you and Zatanna climb down a dark stairway. It opens up into a room filled with rows of fun-house mirrors. The rows twist and turn through the room like a maze.

"I guess this is what the Joker has in store," you say. "We should be careful. We don't know what's behind the mirrors."

There's no reply from Zatanna. You turn around. "Zatanna?"

She's gone.

Now you're worried. Did Zatanna fall into some kind of trap? Or has she been working with the Joker all along? She's the one who called and offered to help, you remember. She's never done that before.

You slowly make your way down the first row of mirrors. You turn a corner and come to a dead end. Your reflection stares back at you—but you can see Zatanna behind you with her hands raised. She's going to attack!

If you break the mirror, turn to page 67.
If you turn and attack Zatanna, turn to page 77.

Continued from page 50.

"I can help if you need it," you say.

Minutes later you drive to an isolated hillside and pull up next to a hero in a red bodysuit. A red mask covers the top half of his face. There's a golden wing on each side of his head. You don't see a vehicle nearby, but that's not surprising. The Flash can run faster than any machine humans are able to build.

"The Justice League is picking up large electromagnetic pulses from this area," the Flash says. "They think this is where the Joker may be keeping the nuclear scientists."

He points to a hole in the hillside. "This tunnel should lead us to them. I could go ahead of you, using my super-speed. If there are any traps, I'll find them."

If you proceed with caution, turn to page 51.
If you send the Flash ahead, turn to page 73.

Continued from page 43.

A few minutes later you pull up in front of the ice cream factory. The sign on the front of the large concrete building has a picture of a smiling ice-cream cone on it. Two squad cars are parked outside.

Blue Beetle climbs out of the Batmobile with you. He's wearing his suit–black-and-blue armor that covers his entire body and head. But it's more than just a suit–it's a living alien being that bonds with Blue Beetle and can communicate with him.

The suit bleeps and lights up. "There are four humans inside," Blue Beetle reports.

"One of them could be the Riddler," you say. You swing open the door.

The whole place is dark. The factory floor is covered with melted ice cream. Chocolate, vanilla, strawberry, pistachio–the flavors swirl on the floor in a big, sticky mess.

Four police officers are wading through the muck.

"You're too late, Batman," says one of the officers. "The Riddler's gone. He cut off the power and now the ice cream's melting."

The officer sounds disappointed.

"Sorry," you say. "I had something else to take care of first."

"We should go after the Riddler," Blue Beetle says eagerly.

The officer frowns. "He's long gone by now."

"If I know the Riddler, he has left us a clue," you say.

You shine your flashlight around the factory. Then you spot something—a note with a green question mark on the front. It's glued to a box of ice-cream cones on a high shelf.

"Got it," Blue Beetle says. He flies up to the shelf and retrieves the note. Then he flies back down and lands next to you.

You take the note and read it out loud.

"Riddle me this, Batman! What's shaped like a square and keeps people cool?"

"An air conditioner!" Blue Beetle says.

"That's a good guess," you agree. "We should head to the air conditioner factory."

"Good luck, Batman!" the police officers call

out as you speed away.

"First ice cream, now air conditioners," Blue Beetle remarks. "Looks like the Riddler is trying to ruin everyone's summer."

"It does," you agree.

But when you arrive at the air conditioner factory, everything is in order. The factory is running smoothly, and the power is still on.

"Sorry, Batman," Blue Beetle says. "I thought I guessed right."

You read the clue again. "Shaped like a square and keeps people cool . . ."

Just then, an alert blares from your police radio. "The Riddler is draining the water from the city pool!"

"The pool! Of course!" you cry.

"It even rhymes," Blue Beetle points out.

The pool is all the way across the city. You want to get there as fast as you can.

If you take the Bat-Copter to beat the Riddler to the pool, turn to page 54.

If you stick with the Batmobile, turn to page 78.

Continued from page 53.

You're so anxious to catch the Joker that you make a rash decision—you and the Flash jump into the nearest Jokermobile.

You hot-wire the green van and quickly zoom out of the garage. Unfortunately, that's as far as you get.

Boom! All four tires explode at once. The van crashes to the ground. You immediately try to open the door, but it's locked tight.

"I can't open mine, either!" the Flash cries.

"It's booby-trapped," you realize. The Joker's loaded it with traps to keep anyone from stealing it.

You know you'll find a way out—but you've lost the Joker's trail.

"We should've taken the Batmobile," you say.

THE END

18

Continued from page 8.

Since the bank robbery is in progress, you decide to go after the Penguin first. You jump into the Batmobile and rev up the engine.

It couldn't hurt to have another hero to back you up. You press a button on the control panel of your dashboard and a small map of Gotham appears. If there are any heroes nearby, your Hero Locator will find them.

Two blinking, green blips appear on the screen. You zoom in on the first blip and see that Huntress is in town. She's sharp and intelligent and a superior athlete. Not only that, but she's a master with a crossbow. But she can be unpredictable sometimes.

You zoom in on the next blip and locate Bronze Tiger. He's a martial arts master with skills that rival yours—but you and he haven't always gotten along.

If you choose Huntress, turn to page 40.
If you choose Bronze Tiger, turn to page 56.

Continued from page 68.

You spin the wheel to the left. It makes a clicking sound as it goes around and around. It slows down, and then finally stops on "Exit."

A trapdoor opens right underneath your feet! You slide down a long, twisting chute. It spits you out onto a cold, concrete floor in a large underground lab.

"Hee hee hee!" You'd recognize the Joker's laugh anywhere. "Looks like the wheel of fortune spun in your favor today, Batman!"

You jump to your feet and take in the scene around you. The Joker is standing next to a large, round vat of what looks like bubbling, green acid. Zatanna is dangling upside down over the vat. There's a black scarf tied over her mouth, and her hands are tied behind her back.

In front of the vat is a carnival game—the kind where you squirt water into the mouth of a clown, and a balloon on the clown gets bigger and bigger. In the game, the first person to pop the balloon wins. Something tells you there's no winner in the Joker's game—except maybe the Joker.

"Let her go, Joker," you say.

"Now why would I do that?" the Joker asks. "I'm about to beat my old friends the Penguin and the Riddler. They were foolish enough to think they could commit crimes more impressive than mine! Those two will never learn."

"What exactly are you planning?" you ask.

"It's beautiful, really," he says. He points across the room, and for the first time you notice two men working on computers. They must be the kidnapped scientists. "These two kind gentlemen have built me a machine that will create a simulated solar flare over all of Gotham City."

"A solar flare would release an incredible electromagnetic charge," you say.

"Looks like somebody got an A in science class," the Joker says. "That's correct. And the electromagnetic charge will wipe out all forms of communication—satellite, radio, cellular—nothing will work!"

The Joker starts giggling maniacally.

"But you won't be able to communicate, either," you point out. Right now, you're stalling for time.

"But I will, Batman," the Joker says. "This entire facility is protected by a Faraday cage, which, as I'm sure you know, redistributes electromagnetic charges. The electromagnetic burst won't penetrate it. I'll be in control of Gotham City!"

You make a move to grab a weapon from your belt—but two of the Joker's minions appear out of nowhere and grab you by the arms. Joker picks up the squirt gun first. He aims it at the clown's mouth, and the balloon starts to inflate.

"Hee hee hee!" he laughs gleefully. "What'll it be, Batman?" he asks. "You can watch the lovely Zatanna drop into this vat of acid. Or, you can surrender to me without a fight. I'll free Zatanna and the scientists, too."

If you surrender, turn to page 48.
If you refuse, turn to page 71.

22

Continued from page 39.

You remove a jet pack from the Batmobile and strap it to your back.

"We'll fly to the rooftop and drop in on the Riddler when he's not expecting it," you say.

"Swoop down like a bat," Blue Beetle says. "I like it!"

Blue Beetle zips up to the top of the building, and you follow with your jet pack. You land on the rooftop and run to a door that leads down into the building. There's a ladder there, and you and Blue Beetle climb down it.

Pow! The Riddler's goons are waiting for you, and one of them clocks you right in the face. Luckily your cowl protects you from the blow. You spin around and take him down with a kick, angry with yourself. The Riddler must have been expecting you to come from the roof.

You punch out another one of the Riddler's henchmen while Blue Beetle takes out the rest with blasts from his jets.

"To the control room!" you say.

Alarms are blaring as you race to the power plant's control room. The Riddler and his goons must have taken out all the workers somehow. When you reach the control room, you find two workers tied up on the floor, but the Riddler is nowhere in sight.

"He ran off when he heard you coming," one of the men says.

"You're just in time," says the other. "He was about to shut down the power."

You and Blue Beetle race back to the rooftop and fly off of the building, searching for any sign of the Riddler. But there's no trace of him.

"At least he didn't shut down the power plant," Blue Beetle says.

He's right—but you wish you had captured the Riddler.

THE END

Continued from page 32.

The Penguin's umbrella has been causing you problems all day. You reach for it first, tossing it across the hideout.

"The Bat is loose!" the Joker cries.

The Riddler attempts to zap you with his question mark–shaped staff, but you jump up and kick it out of his hands.

The Penguin waddles across the hideout, chasing after his umbrella. You press a button on your wrist and a Batarang shoots out, attached to a line. The Batarang flies around the Penguin's legs, and the line wraps around it.

Bam! He falls flat on his face.

"Hee hee hee, Batman! Want to smell my flower?" the Joker asks.

The Joker squeezes the big fake flower on the collar of his green jacket. You know that whatever's going to shoot out of there isn't going to be good.

You quickly grab the Riddler and throw him in the path of the Joker's flower. A green gas floats out and hits the R. . . . falls to the ground in a heap.

The Joker starts to giggle. . . . me, Batman—oh, and the Pengu. . . .

The Joker claps happily as . . . Penguin's goons try to assault you. . . . taken a beating from you and Bronze . . . . . . oday, and they're hurting.

Pow! You clock one in the chin.

Slam! You knock two heads together.

Bam! You jab the last one in the stomach with your elbow. The Joker starts to back up. "It's been fun, Batman, but I think I'll be going now. Here's a little treat for your ride home."

The Joker takes a handful of banana peels out of each pocket and throws them at your feet. You jump over them, somersault in the air, and land right behind the Joker. You quickly pull his hands behind his back and cuff them.

"It takes more than that to slip me up, Joker," you say.

Even though you've made some mistakes, you're pretty pleased with how things worked out. You've captured three villains in one day!

THE END

Continued from page 8.

Of the three villains, the Joker is the most unpredictable—and the most dangerous. The police can probably handle the Penguin for now. You decide to go after the Joker and find those kidnapped nuclear scientists.

Your first step will be to find his hideout. You jump into the Batmobile and head to the Batcave to do some research. As you're driving, your Bat-Phone beeps.

"Hey, Batman, it's Zatanna." Zatanna Zatara is a stage magician with real magical powers she inherited from her father. "Everyone at the club is talking about some crazy contest that the Joker, the Penguin, and the Riddler are having. Do you need some help?"

"Yes," you say without hesitating. You never know what tricks the Joker will have up his sleeve. It could be good to have Zatanna on your side. She's got her own bag of tricks, and they're pretty powerful.

You pick up Zatanna at the nightclub where

she does her act. She's wearing her magician's top hat, tuxedo jacket with tails, a white shirt and bowtie, black shorts, and purple tights. She climbs into the Batmobile.

"Nice to see you, Batman," she says. "So what are we up against?"

"The Joker has kidnapped two nuclear scientists," you reply. "I want to find out where he's hiding them."

"Ooh, so I get to see inside the Batcave?" Zatanna asks eagerly.

"Yes," you say. "I just can't let you see the outside."

You quickly touch a pen to her arm, releasing a sleeping potion. Zatanna's eyes slowly close.

"No . . . fair," she says.

You hate to do it, but it's standard practice for visitors to your hideout. After all, it wouldn't be a hideout if everyone knew where it was.

The sleeping potion doesn't last long. Within a few minutes you and Zatanna are safely inside the Batcave. She's wide-awake and looking at your complex system of computers and gadgets in awe.

"Cool," she says with admiration. "To me, this

stuff is more mysterious than magic."

You call up a blueprint of Gotham City on a large screen. The blueprint shows the entire underground layout of the city. You're looking for an underground space large enough to conduct nuclear experiments.

You quickly locate two possible sites. You zoom in on the first one and click on it, calling up a link to the deed on the property.

"It's a warehouse, owned by somebody named Howie Laff," you read.

"Howie Laff? That sounds like something the Joker would come up with," Zatanna says.

You click on the other space and read the deed for that one. It's a comedy club called the Joke Shack, owned by John Smith.

"Either one could be the front for the Joker," Zatanna says. "The connection's pretty obvious."

"Maybe *too* obvious," you point out. "One could be a trap."

If you go to the warehouse first, turn to page 44.
If you go to the Joke Shack first, turn to page 59.

Continued from page 66.

You strap on a gas mask and throw one to Bronze Tiger. But instead of sleeping gas, snowflake-shaped throwing stars shoot out of the umbrella.

Bronze Tiger does a backflip, avoiding the sharp projectiles. You dodge out of the way, but one hits you in the shoulder.

You immediately start to feel sleepy. The snowflake points must be coated with something, you realize. You pull out the throwing star, but the Penguin's poison is already in your system. As your eyes start to close, you see six henchmen converge on Bronze Tiger.

When you wake up, you're back in the Penguin's headquarters. This time, you find yourself locked in a cage.

"Don't bother reaching for your Utility Belt," the Penguin squawks. "I made sure to remove it this time."

One of the henchmen holds it up, grinning.

"The bars of the cage are titanium steel,"

the Penguin continues. "One hundred percent bat-proof."

"Where's Bronze Tiger?" you ask.

"He got away, but that's just fine," the Penguin replies. "He's just a little fish, Batman. And I've got the biggest fish right here!"

He cackles with glee. Behind him, a large screen lights up. The Joker's face appears—pale white skin, bright green hair, and a hideous grin.

"Hee hee hee hee!" Joker laughs. "I saw your little bank heist on the news, Pengy. Nice work—for an amateur!"

"Why, I oughtta—," Penguin mutters under his breath.

"And the Riddler's ice cream party isn't even worth mentioning," the Joker continues. "Meanwhile, I've created an artificial solar flare that has knocked out all communication in Gotham City! I control it all! I win!"

"Oh, you did, did you?" the Penguin asks.

"Of course," the Joker says with a giggle. "You know the rules, Penguin, my friend. Whoever commits the greatest crime without being captured by Batman wins."

"But what if one of us captures Batman?" the Penguin asks.

"What?" The Joker is clearly surprised.

The Penguin steps to the side to reveal your cage. "Behold, the mighty Batman!"

"Nonsense!" Joker snaps. "That's just one of your henchmen in a costume."

"Batman, say something to the Joker! Prove who you are," the Penguin commands you.

You might be in a cage, but you're nobody's puppet. You stay silent.

"Ha!" the Joker says. "I knew you were lying!"

"He's the real thing, and I'll prove it," the Penguin says. "Come on down and see for yourself."

"Fine!" the Joker shoots back. "And I'll bring the Riddler, too!"

The Penguin walks up to your cage. "Behave yourself, Batman. I've got a contest to win."

"Don't worry, Penguin. I'll stick around," you say. And you mean it. How often do you get a chance to nab the Penguin, the Joker, and the Riddler all at the same time? But first you have to get out of the cage.

The Penguin thinks taking your Utility Belt is pretty smart. But your special Batsuit is equipped for any situation. You slide your fingers under your sleeve and pull out a lock pick. While the Penguin scurries about getting ready for the Joker and the Riddler, you quietly pick the lock.

Then you wait for your moment. In a few minutes, the Joker and the Riddler arrive. The Riddler is in full costume—a purple mask over his eyes and a green jumpsuit covered with black question marks. He's carrying his question mark-shaped staff.

"Hee hee hee!" the Joker laughs when he sees you. "A bat in a trap! Looks like you win after all, Penguin."

That's when you make your move. You burst from the cage. Now you've got to disarm your opponents.

If you get the umbrella away from the Penguin, turn to page 24.

If you grab the Riddler's staff, turn to page 75.

Continued from page 62.

"Blasting through the walls is worth the risk," you say. "I want to be the one who surprises the Riddler this time."

"Sounds good to me," Blue Beetle agrees.

You place a small charge on the wall of the maze. "Stand back," you tell your sidekick.

Boom! The wall crumbles—but the structure of the tunnel is sound. You and Blue Beetle climb through the rubble and find yourselves in a storeroom. There's no trap waiting for you, and none of the Riddler's goons, either.

"The Riddler's probably in the control room," you say.

You race through the hallways of the power plant. The Riddler and his henchmen have tied up all of the workers. When you reach the control room, the Riddler looks shocked to see you.

"Batman! Blue Beetle! How did you get past my traps?" he asks.

You and Blue Beetle quickly grab him.

"Sorry," you say. "Looks like you lose the

contest. I've taken care of the Penguin, too."

"The Joker wins!" the Riddler says. "No fair! I won't have it."

The Riddler tells you exactly what the Joker is planning, and you quickly contact the Flash and give him the information. The Flash catches the Joker, and you're relieved when all three villains are behind bars.

"It's been a long, hot day, Batman," Blue Beetle says. "What do you say we chill out somewhere?"

"A hero's work is never done," you remind him. "But after what we've been through, a little chilling out couldn't hurt!"

THE END

Continued from page 60.

You dive across the room to shield Zatanna. Just as you leap to save her, Zatanna casts a spell to block the flowers.

"LLAF DNA EB SSELPLEH!" she yells.

When Zatanna casts a spell, she speaks a command backward.

It works! The flowers fall to the ground.

And so do you. Everything goes black.

When you wake up, you're sitting in the Batmobile. Zatanna is next to you.

"You got in the way of my spell," Zatanna tells you. "I got you out of there instead of going after the Joker. Now he's knocked out all forms of communication."

"Let me guess," you say. "The Joker is the only one who can communicate, right?"

Zatanna nods. You wish you hadn't jumped in front of her. Now the Joker's got Gotham City in the palm of his hand.

THE END

Continued from page 62.

"Let's try our luck with the door," you suggest. "We'll be ready for him."

You open the door and a shadow passes in front of you. Without thinking, Blue Beetle shoots his lasers at the shadow.

Pieces of the floor begin to sink down around you. You try to keep your balance as you realize you're standing on top of a narrow pole. The drop below you goes farther than you can see.

You scan the situation. There is a pole between you and the door. But Beetle's got nothing around him except empty space.

"Beetle, fly to the door!" you say.

"I'm trying, but I can't," he replies. "There's some kind of electromagnetic pulse in here. It's messing up the suit. Go ahead without me. I'll be fine."

If you go after the Riddler, turn to page 64.
If you help Blue Beetle, turn to page 69.

Continued from page 68.

You spin the wheel to the right. It makes a clicking sound as it goes around and around. It starts to slow down . . . and lands on "Joker Venom."

Joker Venom is the Joker's green gas that leaves his victims paralyzed with a terrible Joker smile. Not good. You quickly slip on an oxygen mask as the gas begins to seep through the walls of the room.

The oxygen mask will buy you some time—but not much. You begin to search the room again.

If you don't find a way out within twenty minutes, you may never get out.

THE END

Continued from page 80.

"All right," you say. "Let's see if we can catch the Riddler at the park before he gets away."

You race to the city park, which isn't far from the pool. People are running out of the park, screaming.

You and Blue Beetle leave the Batmobile and run toward the trees. Leaves are falling to the ground like snowflakes. You look up and see a small army of question mark-shaped blades whirling through the air, slicing leaves as they fly through the trees.

"They must be remote controlled," you say. "If we find the source, we can stop this."

Blue Beetle's suit beeps. "Follow me, Batman!" Blue Beetle says.

Blue Beetle flies off and you follow on foot. He leads you to a green and purple van in a remote corner of the park. A bunch of guys wearing purple jumpsuits are holding remote control devices. Each goon has a different punctuation symbol on his chest: !, #, @, and *.

Blue Beetle immediately starts shooting blasts from the jets under his arms.

Bam! Bam! Bam! Bam! He knocks the remote controls from each of the goons' hands. They scramble to get away.

The van starts up. The Riddler must be behind the wheel! You shoot a grappling hook at the van's rear fender. You want to end this—now.

But the van breaks free with a burst of rocket power, and your hook can't hold on. As the van speeds away, a piece of paper with a question mark on it flutters into your hand. Blue Beetle lands beside you as you open the last clue. "Riddle me this, Batman. What kind of plant doesn't need to be watered?"

"A power plant!" Blue Beetle exclaims. "You were right, Batman. That's his ultimate prize."

You nod. "Let's go!"

When you arrive at the power plant, you see the Riddler's van. You know an underground tunnel you could use to get in. Or you could surprise him with a rooftop entrance.

If you try the rooftop, turn to page 22.
If you go underground, turn to page 61.

Continued from page 18.

Huntress's charm might be just what you need to face the Penguin. You radio her.

"Huntress, the Penguin is robbing Gotham First National Bank. Can you meet me there?" you ask.

A sultry voice replies. "Well, hello to you, too, Batman. Of course I will. You know I can't say no to you."

"Ten-four," you reply.

When you get to the bank, you see the Penguin's goons loading cash into a black-and-white van. Each criminal is dressed alike in black pants, a black turtleneck, and a round, black bowler hat.

You climb out of the Batmobile. Then you hear a voice behind you.

"Ready for action, Batman."

It's the Huntress. She's wearing a purple leotard, long gloves, high black boots, and a mask over her eyes. Her glossy black hair spills onto her shoulders.

"Then let's take down these henchmen," you say.

Huntress scans the scene. "No sign of our tuxedo-wearing friend. Let me flush him out of the van. The last thing we need is a sneak attack from the Penguin's umbrella."

"Good thinking," you admit. "I've got your back."

"I know you do," she says. Then she charges through the henchmen.

The goons are startled. Perfect. You jump into the fray.

Bam! Pow! Slam! You throw punches at the men, ducking to avoid their returning blows. Huntress jumps onto the roof of the van.

A panel on the roof slides open and the Penguin climbs out, holding his umbrella. He doesn't see Huntress behind him. She quickly draws her crossbow and sticks the point of her arrow into his neck.

"Drop the umbrella," the Huntress says, "or you'll never eat another sardine again."

The Penguin obeys.

"Good boy," Huntress tells him. "I'm very disappointed in you, Penguin. What's a refined gentleman like you doing robbing a bank?"

The Penguin is putty in her hands. "You're so right, my lovely Huntress," he says. "Why don't you let me go and I'll show my gratitude by taking you to my favorite seafood restaurant?"

You kick the last standing henchman to the side and jump up onto the van.

"The only food you'll be eating tonight is jailhouse food," you tell the Penguin.

The Penguin frowns. "Batman! You're always spoiling my fun."

"He can't help it," the Huntress tells him. "It's his nature."

You're tired of talking. You cuff the Penguin and take him to the side of the van. The police arrive to help load him and his helpers into a police wagon.

"That wasn't so hard," the Huntress says. "What do you say, Batman? I've got a date, but I'll cancel it. How about a movie?"

"I've got more work to do," you say. "The Joker and the Riddler are both causing trouble."

The radio on your Utility Belt beeps.

"Batman, it's Flash," says your friend. "I heard about the kidnapped nuclear scientists.

I'm on my way to find the Joker. From what I understand, you have your hands full today."

"Thanks, Flash," you say. "Huntress and I have taken care of the Penguin. We'll go after the Riddler and come look for you when we're done."

"Sounds like a plan!" Flash replies.

As he signs off, a flying blue figure swoops down and lands between you and Huntress. It's Blue Beetle!

"Batman, I heard about what the Joker, the Penguin, and the Riddler are doing on the news," says the eager young hero. "I came to help."

"Looks like you're covered, Batman," the Huntress says. "Guess I'll go on my date after all. I'm sure you boys can take care of yourselves."

You turn to the Blue Beetle.

"Thanks for coming," you say. "Now let's go to the ice cream factory!"

Turn to page 14.

Continued from page 28.

There's no logical way to make this decision. You'll just have to choose one or the other and see what happens.

"Let's try that warehouse," you say.

You race through the streets of Gotham City to the warehouse location. It's on the outskirts of town on a deserted street. It doesn't look like anyone's been there for years.

"It's a good place for a secret hideout," Zatanna remarks.

"Could be," you agree.

The warehouse doors are wide open. You enter into a huge room filled with empty steel shelves, dust, and spiderwebs.

"There might be an entrance that leads to the underground lab," you say. "It could be hidden, or it might be in plain sight. You never know with the Joker."

Zatanna nods. "Got it."

You split up and search the warehouse. Then Zatanna calls to you.

"I found another door."

You catch up to her. She's standing in front of a metal door. Unlike everything else in the place, it looks new.

"Could be a trap," you say. "Let me open it."

You turn the door handle . . . and your feet fly out from underneath you! You've triggered a trap.

You fall down, down, down and land on a concrete floor with a thud. Zatanna lands next to you. Your mask and armor have protected you from the fall, but Zatanna's hurt. You check her pulse. She's breathing, but unconscious.

The ceiling slides shut overhead, and you realize you're trapped in a box. There doesn't seem to be a way out. Zatanna could use her magic to get you both out, but she can't do anything while she's knocked out.

For now, you're both trapped.

THE END

Continued from page 53.

"Flash, get the Batmobile," you say.

"Right," the Flash says. Then he's off.

The Flash quickly pulls up in front of the garage. You run to the driver's side.

"What? I can't keep driving?" the Flash asks.

You don't even bother to answer. The Flash sighs and speeds into the passenger seat. Then the two of you take off after the Jokermobile.

In seconds you catch up to the Jokermobile on a deserted stretch of highway. The Joker sees you in his rearview mirror. A green gas pours from the Jokermobile's exhaust.

"Joker Venom," you say. The Joker's dangerous gas is no joke. Luckily, you can cut off exposure to outside air inside the Batmobile.

The Joker tries again. A small trapdoor opens on the back of the van and a barrel of sharp tacks falls out. The tacks would destroy the tires on a normal car, but they harmlessly bounce off the Batmobile's tires.

A nozzle extends from the back of the van,

squirting shaving cream onto the road in front of you. Any other car would skid, but you easily avoid it, driving sideways along the highway guardrail.

Now you're in front of the Jokermobile. You screech to a stop and the Joker spins, trying to turn around. A grappling hook shoots from the Batmobile and attaches to the Jokermobile's back bumper.

Flash speeds from the car and opens the back of the van, freeing the scientists. The Joker opens the van door and makes a run for it, but you quickly shoot a net at him, trapping him.

"Nicely done, Batman," the Joker admits. "But if I can't win, this is the next best thing. I'd rather lose to you than to the Penguin or the Riddler!"

By that night, the story of the villains' contest is all over the news. When you pick up the newspaper the next morning, the headline is impressive: "Batman Captures Three Super-Villains in One Day!"

THE END

Continued from page 21.

Zatanna is in real danger.

"It's a deal, Joker," you say. "I surrender."

You are locked in a cage, but the Joker keeps aiming the water at the clown's mouth.

"Joker! Set her free!" you yell.

"Sorry, I've changed my mind," he says.

Pop! The balloon explodes. But Zatanna has freed her hands, and she pulls the scarf off of her mouth.

"DICA NRUT OT RETAW!"

At her command, the acid turns to water. She splashes safely into the pool.

"SSALG RETTAHS!"

The glass wall around the scientists shatters. Zatanna runs to them and grabs each scientist by an arm.

"TROPSNART!"

All three vanish before your eyes. Zatanna has rescued the scientists. Now all you have to do is get out of this cage!

THE END

Continued from page 80.

"The leaves will grow back," you say. "But if I'm right about the Riddler's plans, we need to make sure we stop him. Take away the power on a hot summer day and the city will fall into chaos."

"Good point, Batman," Blue Beetle agrees.

You race over to the power plant in the Batmobile and park in a spot hidden by bushes. You see workers going about their business. There's no sign of the Riddler anywhere.

"He'll be here soon," you guess. "Let's wait."

Seconds later, a green van with question marks on it pulls up to the power plant gate.

"Now!" you cry.

You and Blue Beetle burst from your hiding spot. Beetle zaps the tires of the van with his jet blasts, and they explode one by one. The back of the van opens up, and the Riddler's goons pour out. While Blue Beetle handles them, you drag the Riddler out of the van.

"Batman! How did you know I

You didn't get the last clue," the Riddler wails.

"You're not that hard to figure out, Riddler," you say.

"Fiddlesticks!" the Riddler cries. "I've got three warehouses filled with ice. I was going to make a fortune selling it to the hot and sweaty citizens of Gotham. But you've foiled my plans."

Four squad cars pull up, and the police officers start handcuffing the Riddler's henchmen. You nod to Blue Beetle.

"Can you make sure he ends up behind bars?" you say with a nod to the Riddler.

"Sure thing, Batman," Blue Beetle says cheerfully. "Glad I could help."

"Thanks, Beetle," you say.

That's two down: the Penguin and the Riddler. Then your radio beeps. It's the Flash!

"I've found the Joker's hideout!"

Turn to page 13.

Continued from page 13.

"I think we should proceed with caution," you say. "If you're traveling at super-speed, you might miss one of the Joker's traps."

"But I've got super-reflexes, too," the Flash points out.

"And I've dealt with the Joker before," you say. "Rushing into things when the Joker's concerned can be dangerous."

"Have it your way," the Flash responds, but you can tell he doesn't agree with you.

The two of you enter the dark tunnel. You illuminate the way with a flashlight. The tunnel is long and filled with twists and turns. You travel about a mile without seeing anything.

"I told you, Batman," the Flash says. "I could have handled this just fine."

You see something glint off your flashlight beam.

"Stop," you say suddenly.

In the light you can just make out the fine strands of some kind of web or net blocking the path ahead of you.

"So—it's a spiderweb," the Flash says. "Big deal."

You slowly approach the web to take a closer look. It's no spiderweb. The strands are tightly woven, like a net. You look up in the corners, where the net attaches to the tunnel walls, and see that it's attached to a round, metal disk.

"I'm guessing that's an alarm," you say. You climb the tunnel walls and carefully dismantle the alarm. Then you cut away the net so you and the Flash can safely pass through.

"You were right, Batman," the Flash admits.

About fifty yards down the tunnel you see a metal door built into the wall. You take a small tube from your belt and press it to the door. Now you can hear everything inside.

"Are you two almost finished with the simulated solar flare?" It's the Joker's voice.

"Soon, Joker, soon," a man responds.

"Once I activate it," the Joker says, "all forms of communication in Gotham City will be knocked out! Hee hee hee! I'll control it all!"

You've heard enough. You nod to Flash and explode the door's lock with a small charge.

Boom! You and the Flash burst into the room. Five of the Joker's goons spring into action, charging you.

Before you can blink, the Flash grabs a long rope from the wall and wraps it around and around the henchmen, trapping all five of them. In the chaos, the Joker leaves with two other henchmen, dragging the scientists behind them.

You chase after them, but when you step through the doorway, a giant inflatable clown pops up in front of you.

Pow! You punch it, but it pops back up.

Frustrated, you slice through it with a bat-shaped blade, deflating it. You're annoyed. You don't have time for the Joker's tricks.

You race down a hall that exits into a garage filled with bright green Jokermobiles. The Joker is speeding away in one of them. The Flash appears next to you.

If you and the Flash jump in one of the Jokermobiles, turn to page 17.

If you send the Flash to get the Batmobile, turn to page 46.

Continued from page 16.

You grab a remote control from your Utility Belt, and in less than a minute the Bat-Copter appears in the sky overhead. It lands in the factory parking lot and you and Blue Beetle climb inside.

You rise into the air and speed toward the city pool as fast as you can. Soon you see the pool below you. People are swimming and splashing in the water. You're not too late!

You begin your descent onto an open baseball field right next to the pool. But you stop before you can reach the ground—something is blocking your way.

Blue Beetle flies out of the passenger seat.

"It's a net!" he shouts over the roar of the engine. "Looks like it's made of some kind of light metal or something."

The Riddler must have been expecting you to fly to the rescue. You try to steer away, but the Copter's landing skids are tangled in the net. The Copter topples over, breaks through the net, and crashes to the ground below.

You can't get out in time and the Copter falls on top of you. You feel a burning pain in your right shoulder and realize it's probably broken. It feels like you've got some broken ribs, too. Blue Beetle appears next to you.

"Batman, are you okay?" he asks.

"I'll be fine," you reply. "Just don't let the Riddler get away."

There's nothing more you can do now. You'll have to let Gotham's other heroes finish this one for you.

THE END

Continued from page 18.

You decide that some extra muscle might be just what you need. You quickly make a left turn and drive to a nearby martial arts dojo. Bronze Tiger is standing outside, talking to some young students.

You roll down the window. "Ben. The Penguin is robbing Gotham First National Bank. I need some backup. You in?"

Bronze Tiger answers by jumping into your passenger seat. The kids watch, wide-eyed, as you zoom away from the curb.

"So what are we up against?" Bronze Tiger asks. Like you, he's got a no-nonsense way of speaking. If there's a job to be done, he'll do it.

"I'm not sure," you reply. "The Penguin, the Joker, and the Riddler have all decided to act up today. I'm taking care of the Penguin first."

You pull up in front of Gotham First National Bank, the Batmobile's brakes squealing. Henchmen wearing black pants, turtlenecks, and bowler hats are loading cash into the back of a van. The Penguin is nowhere in sight.

You and Bronze Tiger jump out of the Batmobile and storm the henchmen.

Pow! You stun one with a punch to the chin.

Slam! Bronze Tiger flips one thief over his shoulder, pounding him into the ground.

You attack the goons so quickly they can't reach for their guns. In minutes, every one of the henchmen is out cold or rolling on the ground in pain.

"Nice work," you tell Bronze Tiger.

Then the roof of the van slides open and the Penguin pokes his head out. As usual, he's dressed in a black–and–white tuxedo and wearing a top hat. A monocle, a round eyeglass lens, is held in place by his right cheek.

"Batman? Who invited you to this party?" the Penguin cackles.

Before you can react, he shoots a spray of gas from his umbrella. You start to cough and sputter.

Then everything goes black.

You wake up upside down. Your feet are bound together and tied to a hook on the ceiling. Your arms are behind your back, and your hands are secured by some kind of metal cuff. A spark tingles on your chin—the cuffs must be electrified.

Looking down, you see a tank below you filled with a white, smoky mist.

"*Kwa, kwa, kwa,*" the Penguin laughs, sounding more like a bird than a human. "That's liquid nitrogen, Batman. When I say the word, you and your friend will drop into the vat and turn into human ice cream pops! A delightful treat on a hot summer day, don't you think?"

"You're a cold-hearted villain, Penguin," you say, but you're really just stalling for time. Behind your back, your fingers fumble with the items on your Utility Belt. You grab onto a small saw, as well as a small taser.

If you use a saw to break through the cuffs, turn to page 63.

If you try to zap the cuffs with a reverse electric charge from the taser, turn to page 65.

Continued from page 28.

There's no logic behind your choice. You've just got to pick one.

"We might as well try the Joke Shack first," you say.

You quickly give Zatanna the sleeping potion as you exit the Batcave and head for the Joke Shack. She wakes up a few minutes before you arrive at the Joke Shack. The comedy club is on a street in a busy part of town, surrounded by restaurants and shops.

You park the Batmobile and walk up to the Joke Shack. The door is open.

"That's odd," Zatanna says. "Most comedy clubs don't open until nighttime."

"Let's be careful," you warn.

You enter the club first. It's empty and quiet. There's a stage on the wall across from you, and it's surrounded by small, round tables and chairs. On the center of each table is a vase with a single fake, yellow flower in it.

"We need to find the entrance to the huge

underground space I saw on the blueprint," you tell Zatanna.

She nods. "Right. I'll check the stage."

Zatanna walks past the tables toward the stage. Suddenly, each fake, yellow flower starts to spin wildly. You realize Zatanna must have triggered something.

The flowers are flying up now, and as you race toward them you can see that their edges are as sharp as knives. Zatanna hears the whirring noise and spins to see what's happening. She raises her hands, like she might be casting some kind of magic spell.

If you dodge the flowers, turn to page 11.
If you shield Zatanna from the attack, turn to page 35.

Continued from page 39.

"We may be able to surprise the Riddler if we take the underground entrance," you tell Blue Beetle. "I'm sure he'll be expecting us to land on the roof."

You make your way through the tangled weeds and bushes in the lot around the power plant. Soon you find an old board on the ground. When you push that aside, there's an old well cover underneath. It's easy to pry off. You and Blue Beetle climb down into the darkness.

When you get to the bottom of the hole, you see the tunnel entrance up ahead. You turn on a flashlight, and Blue Beetle's suit lights up to illuminate the way. After you walk about fifty feet you come to a fork in the path. To your surprise, you see a sign planted in the dirt.

Welcome, Batman! Hope you enjoy this maze I've prepared for you. Your friend, the Riddler.

"Man, that guy thinks of everything," Blue Beetle says.

"He loves to play games," you say.

Blue Beetle's suit beeps. "The suit is doing a scan of the underground maze for us. Look."

The suit projects a hologram from Blue Beetle's chest. It shows the twists and turns of the underground maze. It's shaped like a question mark.

"Whoa," Blue Beetle says.

"Let's go," you tell him.

Thanks to the hologram, it's easy to get through the maze. When you get to the end of the question mark, you come to a door. Blue Beetle starts to open it, but you stop him.

"The Riddler seems to be anticipating our every move," you say. "What if he's expecting us to come through this door?"

"We could blast through these side walls instead," Blue Beetle suggests.

"We could," you agree, "but that might cause the tunnel to collapse around us."

If you blast through the walls of the maze, turn to page 33.

If you go through the door, turn to page 36.

Continued from page 58.

You slip the saw from your Utility Belt and start sawing away at the cuffs. Next to you, Bronze Tiger is struggling to break free.

"Why a bank heist, Penguin?" you ask. "I thought you were trying to impress the Joker and the Riddler. That seems a little boring."

"Well, you see, Batman," the Penguin begins, but then he stops. "What's that sound?"

One of his henchmen points to your hands. "He's trying to saw his way through the cuffs!"

The Penguin frowns. "Enough games, Batman. Freeze them!"

The hooks release you both and you splash into the liquid nitrogen.

Normally, a liquid nitrogen bath would kill you on contact. But Penguin must be using a special formula. You're frozen—you can't move any part of your body—but you're still alive. Unless somebody rescues you and Bronze Tiger, you'll remain living statues forever.

THE END

Continued from page 36.

"I'll come back for you," you tell Blue Beetle.

You jump to the door. When you open it, you see the grinning face of the Riddler.

"Nice of you to drop by, Batman!" he says.

He pushes you backward into the abyss. You plummet and land on top of a kids' bouncy castle.

The castle breaks your fall. A screen lights up on the wall in front of you. Riddler and Joker pop up on the screen.

The Joker looks surprised to see you.

"Say it, Joker," the Riddler says. "Say I win!"

The Joker sighs. "You win."

"When I get out of here, you'll both lose!" you promise.

THE END

Continued from page 58.

You grab for the small taser. If you can produce a negative charge, it may cancel out the positive charge of the cuffs.

"Tell me something, Penguin," you say, trying to distract him. "Why a bank heist? I thought you were trying to impress the Joker and the Riddler with a huge crime."

"Oh, but that's just the first step, Batman," the Penguin says. "Soon, I'll empty out every bank in Gotham City. I will own this town!"

You quickly press the taser to the cuffs.

Buzz! The cuffs snap open. Hands free, you swing up and untie the straps around your feet.

"Stop him!" the Penguin cries.

A henchman rushes toward you. You throw a Batarang at him, sending him flying backward.

You have just enough time to free Bronze Tiger. You pivot toward him and zap the cuffs around his hands. Then you jump over the tank and land on the floor.

The Penguin and his henchmen scramble out

of the hideout. Bronze Tiger jumps down next to you. Without a word, you give chase.

The Penguin and his crew jump into the van and speed off before you can catch up. You press a button on your Utility Belt to summon the Batmobile. You're losing valuable time.

"What's taking so long?" Bronze Tiger growls at you.

Just then the Batmobile pulls up to a stop in front of you. You shoot Bronze Tiger a triumphant look. Then you jump inside.

You have a feeling you know where the Penguin is headed. The closest bank to your current location is less than a mile away.

When you reach the bank, Penguin is standing outside the van.

"Curses, Batman!" he says, pointing his umbrella at you.

Does the umbrella contain more sleeping gas, or another dangerous surprise? You have to defend yourself—quickly.

If you whip out your Bat Shield, turn to page 9.
If you put on a gas mask, turn to page 29.

Continued from page 12.

You realize that you trust Zatanna a lot more than you trust the Joker. Guessing that the image in the mirror is an illusion, you smash it with your fist. Glass shatters all around you.

You look back, and Zatanna is nowhere to be seen. In front of you is a dark passage. With luck, it will lead to the Joker and the two kidnapped scientists. Wherever Zatanna is, you hope she's safe.

A flashlight illuminates the narrow path as you make your way down. You turn left, turn right, then turn left again. You're starting to wonder if the passage leads anywhere at all.

Finally, you come to a metal door. To your surprise, it's unlocked. You slowly open it to reveal a pitch-black room.

You step inside and the door slams shut behind you. Bright light suddenly fills the space. You whirl around and see that the door is gone! In fact, there doesn't seem to be a door on any of the walls in the small room. The only thing in sight is a large wheel, the kind you'd find at a carnival stand. But you can't win a stuffed animal by spinning this one. And the spaces around the wheel aren't filled with numbers or letters. Instead, they're filled with options like "Find the Exit" and "Joy Buzzer."

Spinning that wheel is the last thing you want to do. You make a careful search of the room, looking for a way out, but you find nothing. You look at the wheel and sigh. If you ever want to get out of the room, you're going to have to spin.

If you spin the wheel to the left, turn to page 19.
If you spin the wheel to the right, turn to page 37.

Continued from page 36.

You're not about to leave Blue Beetle here by himself. There's got to be a way to save him without getting into a jam yourself.

You use your flashlight to scan the underground space. That electromagnetic pulse is a problem that needs to be solved. It's got to be coming from somewhere . . .

Then you see it—a small, black device hidden in the corner of the room. You reach for a bat-shaped throwing star and aim it at the device. It explodes in a shower of sparks.

Blue Beetle's suit beeps. "Hey, the suit's happy again," Beetle reports.

"Then meet me at the door," you say.

Blue Beetle flies to the door, and you jump from pole to pole to get there.

Bam! The two of you kick in the door.

To your surprise, the Riddler is right behind it! He goes flying backward. He's surprised to see you and Blue Beetle, too.

You quickly charge the Riddler and cuff his

hands behind his back.

"Nice try, Riddler," you say. "But not good enough."

Your radio beeps. It's the Flash.

"Batman! I've got the Joker in custody. The nuclear scientists are safe," he reports.

"Good work," you say.

"Hey, that means all three villains are captured," Blue Beetle says. "Cool."

"I couldn't have done it without you," you say. "Thanks!"

THE END

Continued from page 21.

"I'll never surrender!" you cry.

Bam! You jab each goon holding you with your elbow. They double over, groaning.

Pop! The balloon on the carnival game bursts just as Zatanna breaks free of her bonds.

"DICA NRUT OT RETAW!"

The acid turns to water, and Zatanna splashes into the vat.

Three more goons assault you. You take care of them as quickly as you can.

Pow! Wham! Ker-bam!

Zatanna says another spell.

"SSALG RETTAHS!"

The glass room shatters around the trapped scientists. You look up to see that Zatanna has each one by an arm.

"I can get them out of here," she tells you.

You nod. "I've got the Joker!"

"TROPSNART!"

Zatanna and the scientists vanish. All of the Joker's goons are on the ground, groaning.

"Impressive, Batman," the Joker admits. "But I'm not through playing yet!"

He tosses a smoke bomb at you. You immediately start to cough and choke. You can't see more than an inch in front of you.

You quickly put on your heat-vision goggles. Now you can see the outline of the Joker's body through the smoke. He's trying to escape through a trapdoor. But you jump up behind him, grabbing him by the neck.

"Sorry, Joker," you say. "You lose."

Outside, Zatanna has marshaled the police. You turn over the Joker to Commissioner Gordon.

"It's been quite a day, Batman," he tells you. "The police have captured the Penguin and the Justice League just brought in the Riddler."

"Nice work, Batman," Zatanna says. "We should go somewhere and celebrate."

"Where do you have in mind?" you ask.

She smiles. "Anywhere but a comedy club!"

THE END

Continued from page 13.

Sending the Flash ahead to check for traps sounds like a good idea to you.

"All right," you say. "I'll wait here."

The Flash zooms into the tunnel, a blur of red. He's not gone long when you hear a loud alarm start beeping in the tunnel.

You know if everything's all right, you'll see the Flash in seconds. But you don't. You've got no choice now—you've got to enter the tunnel.

You use a flashlight to make your way through the dark passage. After a mile, there's still no sign of the Flash.

Finally, you spot him. He's tangled in an almost invisible net that's hanging from the ceiling.

"Sorry, Batman," the Flash says. "I was going so fast I didn't see it."

You take out a knife and quickly cut him down. "No problem. At least we know we're in the right place."

You and the Flash proceed through the rest

of the tunnel with caution. There are no more traps. You come to a large, metal door. It's locked, but you're able to open it by blasting the lock with a small, explosive charge.

Once the door opens, you and the Flash burst into the room. You're in some kind of lab, but it's empty.

"The alarm must have tipped off the Joker that we were here," you say.

"I'll find him!" the Flash says. He speeds off again, returning seconds later.

"Looks like the Joker got away with the two scientists," he reports. "They must have moved quickly after that trap went off. I lost their trail."

You're not happy. If you were able to choose again, you'd go through the tunnel carefully, not quickly.

THE END

Continued from page 32.

You grab the Riddler's question mark-shaped staff and throw it across the room. Then you turn to the Penguin.

Zap! A crooked laser blast shoots from the point of the umbrella. The laser hits you, paralyzing you.

Not again! you think as your eyes close against your will.

"Welcome to the Museum of Heroes! Step right up to see our latest attraction—the one and only Batman!"

You slowly open your eyes and realize you still can't move. The Joker is talking into a megaphone and leading a small crowd of villains toward you. Behind them, more villains are forking over wads of cash.

You move your eyes from side to side and see that you're standing in a cheesy replica of the Batcave. The walls are made of gray-painted Styrofoam. A computer made of cardboard and aluminum foil stands against the side wall.

"Here's what you paid your money for, folks," the Joker says. "The mighty Batman in his natural environment. Proof that I am the greatest villain of all time!"

Penguin angrily waddles over. "What are you talking about, Joker? I'm the one who captured Batman!"

The Riddler jumps between them. "Riddle me this, fellows! Why couldn't the Joker and the Penguin be the greatest villains ever? Because I am!"

You're not sure what's more annoying—not being able to move, or having to listen to these three losers argue. You just hope that Bronze Tiger is looking for you. Without help, you probably won't be able to escape.

THE END

Continued from page 12.

You quickly spin around and hurl a Batarang at Zatanna. A look of shock crosses her face.

"Batman, what are you—"

Bam! The Batarang hits her, knocking her off her feet. She skids backward across the floor, crashing into the wall of mirrors.

Zatanna wasn't expecting your attack, which is why she didn't cast a spell to stop you. Puzzled, you look back in the mirror.

The image of Zatanna is still there. She starts to cackle with laughter—and she sounds exactly like the Joker.

"Hee hee hee hee hee!"

Then the image fades, and you realize you've been tricked! The image of Zatanna attacking you was only an illusion.

You rush to Zatanna's side, and you realize she's badly hurt. You carry her back to the Batcave to tend to her injuries. You'll have to go after the Joker later—if it's not too late.

THE END

Continued from page 16.

You and Blue Beetle jump into the Batmobile. You zoom through the streets of Gotham City. But it's a nice summer day and the streets are crowded with people. It takes longer than you wanted to reach the city pool.

When you arrive, you find a crowd of angry people in bathing suits gathered around the large pool. You and Blue Beetle jump out of the Batmobile to investigate. When the crowd sees you, people start shouting.

"Somebody drained all the water from the pool!" someone complains.

"It was the Riddler," says a little girl. "I saw him!"

"We're too late!" Blue Beetle cries.

"The Riddler planned it that way," you say. "That's why he made his first clue so vague—to get us offtrack."

"There must be another clue around here somewhere," Blue Beetle says.

"If there is, we'll find it," you promise him.

You split up. More people come up to you to complain. They all seem to think you can somehow fill the pool yourself.

"I'm sure the good people at the parks department will get the pool filled soon," you say. "In the meantime, you'll have to find some other way to stay cool."

"But the ice cream truck is out of ice cream!" a little boy wails. A bunch of kids start crying.

The Riddler is starting to impress you. He's found a way to make everyone in Gotham City miserable. That's no small feat.

Then you see some kids on the side of the pool hitting a beach ball around. The beach ball has white and green stripes and is decorated with black question marks.

You freeze. It's the sign of the Riddler! The clue is probably inside, which means the ball is about to explode!

"I'm on it, Batman!" Blue Beetle cries. He zips by you in a flash of blue. He grabs the beach ball and carries it over to the empty pool.

Boom! The beach ball explodes in his hands, but Blue Beetle is protected by his suit. He's left holding a piece of paper. Blue Beetle flies to you and gives you the clue.

Riddle me this, Batman! When does a tree say good-bye?

"When it *leaves*!" Blue Beetle says, solving the riddle. "That's pretty lame. What does it mean?"

"The leaves on a tree give people shade," you reason. "Many of Gotham's good citizens seek shade in the city park."

"I bet the Riddler is going to steal the leaves from the trees!" Blue Beetle guesses. "We should hurry."

But you have another thought. "If we're going to beat the Riddler, we have to stay one step ahead of him," you say. "He's taking away everything that keeps people cool. Eventually, he's going to try to cut the power in the city. Maybe we should go right to the power plant."

"But if we do that, all the trees in the park will lose their leaves!" Blue Beetle reminds you.

If you go to the park, turn to page 38.
If you go to the power plant, turn to page 49.